Mookie Is Missing!

Carol Ghiglieri

SCHOLASTIC INC.

New York Toronto London Auckland Sydney
Mexico City New Delhi Hong Kong Buenos Aires

**Illustrations
Monika Melnychuck**

ISBN 0-439-69867-7

4   5   6   7   8   9   10   23   12 11 10

Contents

What's making all that noise
in the middle of the night?

1

A Sleepless Night

Screech, bang, bong, bang!

Lizzie woke with a start. What were those strange noises coming from the apartment upstairs?

Lizzie lived on the 17th floor of the Zoo Arms apartment building. It was right across the street from the zoo.

It was the perfect location for Lizzie

Lizzie woke with a start. What were those strange noises?

because she loved the zoo. In fact, she'd been working as a volunteer there all summer. She worked in the **Primate Pavilion**, taking care of a zillion kinds of monkeys. Tomorrow was her last day, and she was sad the job was almost over.

The noises from upstairs had stopped, but Lizzie couldn't get back to sleep. She climbed out of bed and stared out her window at the zoo.

Suddenly, something caught Lizzie's eye. A silver van with a big Z on the roof was leaving the zoo parking lot. It was the zoo's van, but only Ms. Ramsey, the zoo director, drove it.

That's strange, Lizzie thought. *Why is Ms. Ramsey working so late?*

primate any member of the group of animals that includes monkeys, apes, and humans
pavilion one of a group of buildings

Lizzie saw a silver van with a big *Z* on it leaving the zoo parking lot.

What a weird night, Lizzie thought. Then she got back in bed and went to sleep.

What do you think is making the noise upstairs?

Lizzie slips on a banana peel.
Will anything else go wrong today?

2

Mookie Is Missing!

The next morning Lizzie was tired, but she got up and got ready for her last day at the zoo. She was looking forward to seeing Mookie, her favorite gorilla. She thought Mookie was definitely the cutest and smartest of all the gorillas.

After Lizzie got dressed, she rode the elevator down to the Zoo Arms lobby.

On her way out of the elevator, she slipped on something and fell.

Bam! She landed flat on her back.

She got up and looked to see what she had stepped on. "A banana peel!" she said. "Some people are such animals!"

Just then, Jimmy, the building's **handyman**, walked through the lobby. Lizzie picked up the peel and showed it to him.

"Where'd that come from?" Jimmy asked.

"Some animal dropped it," Lizzie said, as she yawned.

"You look **exhausted**," Jimmy said.

"That new guy upstairs was making lots of noise last night," Lizzie told him.

handyman someone who fixes things
exhausted very, very tired

"I think he's a scientist, so maybe he was doing some kind of experiment," Jimmy said. "He's kind of strange, if you want my opinion."

Lizzie crossed the street and showed her zoo pass to Anne McHenry, the zoo's ticket taker.

"*Achoo!*" Anne sneezed. As Anne reached for a tissue to blow her nose, Lizzie noticed a big scratch on her arm.

"What happened to you?" Lizzie asked, pointing to the scratch.

"Oh, it's just a little scratch," Anne said. "My cat did it." Anne sneezed again.

"Are you okay?" Lizzie asked. "You don't sound good."

"It's just a cold, so it's really no big

"What happened to you?" Lizzie asked when she saw Anne's arm.

deal," Anne said. "But have you heard the news?"

"What news?" Lizzie asked.

Just then Ms. Ramsey, the zoo director, ran up to Lizzie and Anne. "Mookie is missing!" she cried. "Someone took Mookie!"

*The clues start to add up . . . and they
lead straight to the Zoo Arms!*

3

On Mookie's Trail

Lizzie was **devastated**. How could someone steal Mookie?

Lizzie knew she had to find the gorilla, but that might take some energy—and some planning. So she decided to get some ice cream first. At the Zoo Café, she bought a cone, sat on a bench, and started thinking about what to do.

devastated shocked and upset

Lizzie and Anne sat on a bench and planned how to find Mookie.

A minute later, Anne sat down next to her and started eating a box of raisins.

"I can't believe somebody stole Mookie," Lizzie said.

"Maybe he wasn't stolen," Anne said. "Maybe he ran away. He's really smart, you know." Anne often said that Mookie could be the star of his own TV show. "Maybe he figured out how to escape."

"I doubt it," said Lizzie. "Mookie is smart all right, but I think he likes it here." She licked her ice cream cone.

"What flavor do they have today?" Anne asked.

"Banana chocolate chip," Lizzie said.

"Aw, that's Mookie's favorite," said Anne. Then she sneezed again.

"Wait! I just thought of something," said Lizzie. She remembered the banana peel in the elevator, and then she thought about the screeching in the apartment upstairs.

"You know what, Anne?" Lizzie said. "I think I know where Mookie is!"

Anne dropped her box of raisins, spilling them all over the ground.

"You do?" she choked.

"Yes, I do!" Lizzie said.

"Where?" Anne asked.

"In the apartment above mine," Lizzie said. "I have to get in there!"

"I'll go with you," Anne said.

Then they both jumped up and ran to the Zoo Arms.

Lizzie goes to visit her neighbor
and hopes that she'll find Mookie.

4

A Man With a Peel

Anne and Lizzie ran all the way up to the 18th floor and knocked on the door of the apartment above Lizzie's.

The man who opened it wasn't much taller than Lizzie. He was bald and wore glasses—and he was eating a banana!

"Hello!" he said. "May I help you?"

"Hi," Lizzie said, panting. "I'm Lizzie.

I live downstairs, and this is my friend Anne. We both work at the zoo."

"Well, well," said the man. He finished his banana and then tossed the peel behind him. "My name is Dr. Dalton. Please come in."

Dr. Dalton's apartment was a huge mess. In the center of his living room, there was a big workbench covered with toys. In fact, there were toys everywhere.

"In case you were wondering," the man said, "I'm a toy maker."

"You are?" Lizzie's eyes grew wide. "That's pretty cool."

"This is a toy I just made." Dr. Dalton pointed to a two-foot-high **mechanical** gorilla and flipped a switch. The gorilla

---

mechanical operated by machinery

The mechanical gorilla stomped across the floor, screeching loudly.

stomped across the floor, screeched loudly, and then fell over with a bang.

"Dang it!" said Dr. Dalton. "That keeps happening."

Lizzie stared at the toy. "So that's what I heard last night." She whispered to Anne, "It looks like Dr. Dalton didn't steal Mookie after all."

Anne didn't seem so sure. "He still seems kind of **suspicious**, if you ask me."

Lizzie turned to Dr. Dalton. "Did you know a gorilla is missing from the zoo?"

"Who would steal a gorilla?" he asked.

"Yeah," said Anne. "Who would?"

Lizzie looked out the window and saw a silver van driving by on the street below.

She turned to Anne, excited. "Anne,

suspicious unusual; leading you to think that something is wrong

I just thought of something," Lizzie said. "Last night, I couldn't sleep, and I was staring out of my window. I saw Ms. Ramsey driving away from the zoo!"

Anne seemed upset. "You did?" she asked anxiously. "Are you sure you weren't dreaming?"

"I definitely wasn't dreaming," Lizzie said. "And it was definitely the zoo van."

Suddenly Anne looked at her watch. "Listen, Lizzie, I've got to go. I have the afternoon off, so I won't be going back to the zoo with you."

Then Anne ran out the door without even saying good-bye.

Lizzie turned to Dr. Dalton. "That was weird," she said. "But I should be leaving,

Anne left Dr. Dalton's apartment without even saying good-bye.

too. It was nice to meet you and your toys, Dr. Dalton. Good luck fixing your gorilla."

Why is Lizzie no longer suspicious of Dr. Dalton?

Lizzie is starting to wonder—did the zoo director steal the zoo's gorilla?

5

Another Suspect

Lizzie went back to the zoo and found Ms. Ramsey in the Primate Pavilion.

"Hello, Ms. Ramsey," Lizzie said. "Is there any news about Mookie?"

"No, there's not," Ms. Ramsey sighed. "And none of the guards noticed anything suspicious last night."

"Well, *I* saw something suspicious,"

Lizzie told her.

Ms. Ramsey gasped. "You did?"

"I saw you pulling out of the zoo parking lot at midnight!" Lizzie said.

"That's impossible!" Ms. Ramsey said. "I was home asleep."

"Well, I'm sure it was the zoo van," Lizzie said. "I saw the big *Z* on the roof."

"Are you saying I took Mookie?" Ms. Ramsey demanded.

"No, I'm just saying I saw the van pulling out of the parking lot. Does anyone else have the keys?" Lizzie asked.

"I don't think so," she said, "But wait— Anne has a **spare** set of keys because I let her use the van when her car was in the shop. Now that I think about it, I don't

spare extra

"Anne never came back from her lunch break!" Ms. Ramsey told Lizzie.

think she ever returned the keys."

"Could Anne have taken the van last night?" Lizzie said.

"I guess so," Ms. Ramsey said slowly.

"And Anne had that scratch on her arm this morning!" Lizzie said. "She said her cat gave it to her."

"Anne doesn't even have a cat!" Ms. Ramsey said. "She's **allergic** to animal hair!"

"She was sneezing her head off this morning!" Lizzie said. "Plus, she knew Mookie's favorite ice cream flavor—and she doesn't even work with the primates."

"And she's supposed to be working the gate this afternoon," Ms. Ramsey said. "But she never came back from lunch!"

allergic made sick by

Lizzie looked surprised. "She told me she had the afternoon off!" she exclaimed.

Ms. Ramsey grabbed Lizzie's hand, and they ran to the silver van. As they sped out of the parking lot, Ms. Ramsey tossed her cell phone to Lizzie. "Call the police," she ordered, "and tell them to meet us at Anne's house as soon as possible."

Do you think that Ms. Ramsey and Lizzie will find Mookie at Anne's house? Why or why not?

Lizzie thinks she knows where Mookie is.
Will she be right this time?

Primate Rescue

Lizzie and Ms. Ramsey pulled into Anne's driveway just as the police arrived. They all ran to Anne's door and banged loudly, but she did not answer.

Then they heard a noise coming from the backyard. They all ran to the back. Anne was trying to lead a gorilla into a truck—and that gorilla was Mookie!

Lizzie ran over to Mookie. The gorilla gave her a hug.

"Stop right there, Anne McHenry," a police officer yelled.

Anne turned around. Her jaw dropped, and her face went white.

"That gorilla belongs in the zoo!" Lizzie said.

"You little gorilla freak!" Anne screamed at Lizzie.

Lizzie ran over to Mookie, and he gave her a hug.

"I missed you, Mookie," Lizzie said.

The police officers handcuffed Anne.

"Anne, why did you do it?" Ms. Ramsey asked.

"That gorilla was going to make me rich," Anne said. "A TV producer in Los Angeles offered me a lot of money for

Mookie. And I would have gotten away with it, if it wasn't for Lizzie—that big gorilla freak!"

After school the next day, Lizzie went to the Primate Pavilion to visit Mookie. He was playing happily with his friends. Ms. Ramsey was there, too.

"Lizzie, how was your first day of school?" Ms. Ramsey asked.

"It was great," Lizzie said. "I'm already planning to do a report on gorillas."

"I guess that means you'll need to do a lot of research," Ms. Ramsey said.

"That's right," said Lizzie. "You and Mookie will be seeing a lot of me."

Glossary

allergic *(adjective)* made sick by

devastated *(adjective)* shocked and upset

exhausted *(adjective)* very, very tired

handyman *(noun)* someone who fixes things

mechanical *(adjective)* operated by machinery

pavilion *(noun)* one of a group of buildings

primate *(noun)* any member of the group of animals that includes monkeys, apes, and humans

spare *(adjective)* extra

suspicious *(adjective)* unusual; leading you to think that something is wrong